L B

Little, Brown and Company
New York   Boston

for ED

ABOUT THIS BOOK

The illustrations for this book were created using Chinese ink, watercolor, gouache, and colored pencil, as well as materials salvaged from a falling-down nineteenth-century farmhouse in New York State: wallpaper, composition books, newspapers, brown-paper bags, clothing, handkerchiefs, curtains, and string. This book was edited by Susan Rich and designed by Sophie Blackall, David Caplan, and Prashansa Thapa. The production was supervised by Ruiko Tokunaga, and the production editor was Jen Graham. The text was set in Old Claude LP.

Farmhouse

Sophie Blackall

Over a hill,
at the end of a road,
by a glittering stream
that twists and turns,
stands a house

where twelve children
were born and raised,
where they learned to crawl
in the short front hall,
where they posed, arranged
on the wooden stairs,
and were measured with marks
over the years,

where they carved potatoes
and dipped them in paint
to pattern the walls
with flowers and leaves,
and painted the cat,
about which they lied,

for which they were scolded
and maybe they cried
and then were enfolded
in forgiving arms
in the serious room
(where the organ was played
and speeches were made),
but if they weren't
even sorry at all,
they were sent to their rooms,

where they pored over books
about planets and stars,
then climbed into beds
where they dreamed of Mars
(or they dreamed of cats
or the distant sea)

and whispered secrets,
played truth or dare,
and lost their teeth
and brushed their hair,
where they kept collections
of tin toy cars
and feathers and bones
and movie stars,
where they hung prize ribbons
for champion cows
that lived in the barn
behind the house

and were milked twice a day no matter the weather,

at dawn and at dusk by one child or another,

who shivered and grumbled as they crossed the yard

or liked being alone with a flaming cloud,

depending on the season, the day, and the child,

and they fed the calves
and mucked out stalls
and forked the hay
into giant piles
and fished for trout
in the glittering stream
that changed its shape
from year to year,

and walking home
with their rods and flies,
they picked gnarled apples
to turn into pies,

and dragged in mud
from the fields outside,
so they shook the rug
and scrubbed the floors
and listened to their mother
and did their chores
and set the table

and bowed their heads
and dished up soup
and tore up bread

and took turns tending the youngest one,

who lay with a fever and a spotted tongue,

and as they watched, they darned their socks

and sewed on buttons that once were shells

in the faraway sea that they'd never seen,

and they waited for spring,

which eventually came,

as it did every year,

with blossoms and rain,

which leaked through the holes

that had grown in the roof,

collecting in bowls and pans and pails,

staining the wall in the short front hall

with the flowers and leaves

and measures and marks

from the children who all
grew up in this house,
who went off to school
or to work on a farm,
or to drive a truck
or train as a nurse,
or study the stars
or have babies themselves,
until one day,
the youngest child,
who was now quite old,
took a last look around
and picked up her case
and opened the door

and stepped outside
and into a car,
where her sister was waiting,
to drive to the sea,
which they'd always,
always wanted to see,

and the house
gave a sigh
and slumped
on the stones,
which caused
a slight lean
in its beams
and its bones,
so the door
swung open
to let in
the breeze

and welcomed the rain

that rotted the floor,

where a sapling grew

right next to the stove,

where the wallpaper peeled

like onion skins

and drifted about

with the fallen leaves

and the button that was once

a shell in the sea,

by the parlor organ

that rattled with nuts,

put there by a squirrel

with rather a fuss,

which startled the swallows

that fed on the moths

that fluttered and flew

all over the house—

there was even a bear

in the basement one year,

who slept there all winter

until the spring,

which was when I came
and cut a path
through prickly burdock
and nettles and grass
and found what remained
of the old farmhouse,
where I filled my arms
with wallpaper scraps
and rain-soaked books
and brittle maps
and mud-caked dresses
and handkerchiefs
and a button
that was once a shell in the sea,

and back at my desk,
I spread them all out
and cherished my gifts
from the falling-down house,
then I sharpened my pencil
and mixed some paint
and dipped my brush
and cut some shapes
and began to imagine
the things that took place

in the home where twelve children were born and raised, where they ate and slept
and worked and played and laughed and loved and grew quite old,

where they'll live on, now, in this book that you hold,

like your stories will, so long as they're told.

AUTHOR'S NOTE

I have always loved old things. Especially old, worn, mended things that show traces of hands and hearts and minds long gone, things that tell stories. Like a china doll with one hand-carved wooden arm, or much-darned stockings that once covered feet that must have walked miles.

Imagine my excitement, then, to buy an old farm that came with a falling-down house where twelve children were born and raised—a house filled with scraps and fragments that helped me imagine the lives lived within its walls.

I first explored the house on a late-spring day. Outside, the meadow was noisy with chattering birds, and the wildflowers nodded their heads in the sun. Inside, everything was cool and dark and quiet. The floor was scattered with brittle leaves, a saucepan lid, and a stiff leather shoe. An ornate parlor organ held walnut shells and the curled-up pages of lovesick songs. A waterlogged catalog offered beehives and waffle irons, bedsprings and guitar strings. In the kitchen, newspapers, with reports of milk prices and war, lined sagging pantry shelves of rusted tin cans. A straw mattress slumped in a corner. A calendar still hung on the wall, open to July 1970, the month and year I was born.

A willow sapling grew through a hole in the floor, reaching toward a hole in the roof. Nobody had lived there for a long time. Well, no people, that is. Plenty of animals had taken shelter. Raccoons, judging by the droppings; squirrels, by the walnut shells; swallows, by the nests. Not to mention mice and bats and wasps. It was as well I didn't know, until a farmer told me later, that a bear had been sleeping in the basement.

I was convinced then and there that I needed to honor this farmhouse. Even though it was falling down and beyond repair. Even though there were houses just like it collapsing across the countryside, as small dairy farms sold their cows and gave up fighting to survive in a changing world. Even though, several months from now, a roaring excavator would come and extend its long neck and open its wide jaws, bite through the beams, push over

the walls, crunch up the parlor organ, and bury it all ten feet underground. But before that time, there were stories to collect.

I salvaged a bird's nest, a handkerchief and a wedding dress, the farmhouse front door, an old brass key, and a button that was once a shell in the sea. In the autumn, I carried out a pile of mud-caked rags, which turned out to be twenty-one handmade dresses. I separated them and hung them in an old apple tree to dry. Fused clumps of wallpaper soaked in warm water revealed layers of vibrant patterns. I teased apart moldy pages of schoolbooks and learned something of the personalities of the Swantak children born in this house.

Many of the descendants of the Swantak family still live in the valley, and they were incredibly generous with their recollections and stories and scrapbooks. As I was piecing together the history of the farmhouse, I also spoke to eighth-generation local farmers and delved into researching the history of the area before their arrival, and continue to learn about the Haudenosaunee, the original custodians of this part of upstate New York.

After the digger had buried the house and rumbled away, and the clearing was quiet, I crouched in the middle of the tamped-down earth and emptied my pockets of handfuls of seeds. I hoped that next spring wildflowers would grow—poppies and lupines and Queen Anne's lace—in the rich soil made of layers of stories, stretching back to the beginning of time.

The pictures in this book are made of layers. I began with the reverse side of a roll of wallpaper and added floors and walls and furniture, made from scraps and fragments I found in the house. Most of the first layers are invisible now, hidden beneath embellishments and details, in the way that stories become layered as they get told and retold over the years. Stories about everything, and nothing much, that stay alive long after children grow up and houses fall down, while wildflowers nod their heads in the sun.